GW01003814

Maximus

goes on holiday

© 1996 Scripture Union
Text copyright © 1996 Brian Ogden
Illustrations copyright © 1996 Elke Counsell
First published 1996.

Scripture Union, 207–209 Queensway,
Bletchley, Milton Keynes MK2 2EB, England.

ISBN 1 85999 058 4

All rights reserved.

Designed by Tony Cantale Graphics.

Printed in Singapore by Tien Wah Press.

Maximus
goes on holiday

Brian Ogden

Illustrated by Elke Counsell

Scripture Union

'Four pairs of socks, trainers, towels, T shirts, trousers, toothbrush and paste, what else should I take? Will I have enough socks – perhaps I should take another pair?' asked Maximus.

Maximus was going on holiday and Patrick and Paula were helping him to pack his case. They had already told him he wouldn't need a week's supply of hymnburgers so these had to come out of the case before the clothes went in. Maximus was going to America to visit his cousins who had gone to live there. He had never flown before and he was getting very excited.

'There can't be many mice that fly to America,' boasted Maximus. 'I am a bit special, you know.'

'Don't forget a sun hat – it can get very hot in America,' said Paula, ignoring Maximus. The hat was added to the pile of clothes waiting to go in the case. When it was full, Patrick and Maximus jumped up and down on it, whilst Paula did up the lock.

'You're quite sure I have everything I need?' said Maximus. 'It is important that I look very smart. There simply aren't many flying mice, you know.'

As they left the church, Maximus spoke to Barnabas the bat.

'Just off to America, Barnabas. Can't hang around gossiping – must fly! I'm flying on Conker, you know.'

'Maximus – it's actually Concorde,' said Patrick.

As Maximus got into the taxi to take him to the station, Robert and his family of rabbits hopped past.

'I'm off to the Useless of A,' he said. 'Going to visit my cousin Tex.'

'Er, Maximus, it's actually the U.S. of A. Meaning United States of America,' corrected Paula.

'Well, never mind,' said Maximus. 'Bye, you two. Bet you wish you were coming with me?'

A few hours later Maximus arrived at the airport, handed over his case and went through the door into the Departure Lounge.

Please let this mouse go on holiday.

Maximus Mouse

'That really is me,' he said to the Custom's Officer, pointing to his passport photograph. 'I know it doesn't look much like it. I'm going to America – flying you know.' It was a rather old photograph, taken when Maximus wore his hair in punk style. He sat down in a very large lounge with comfortable chairs and a television screen which told about all the flights. There were planes going everywhere it seemed.

Maximus saw that there was still over an hour to wait before the flight and wandered over to the Tiny Cook café. He looked at all the food and ordered a Big Max burger.

'I'm flying on Conker to America, you know,' he said, as he paid for his burger. 'Don't suppose you meet many famous mice like me!'

He went back to his seat and watched other planes take off and land as he ate. Two white mice came and sat next to him.

'I'm flying to America,' said Maximus. 'Get around quite a lot you know, I do.'

'That's nice,' said the lady mouse. 'And what part of America?'

'My cousin Tex lives in Mouseville, Collectacat. He works in films in Hollywood – does the stunt work for

Jerry in the Tom and Jerry cartoons. 'Spect he'll take me to Hollywood to meet all the film stars.'

At that moment there was an announcement.

'Would all passengers flying to New York on Concorde please go to Gate Six.'

Maximus' heart missed a beat.

'Bye then, have a good holiday,' said the white mice.

But as Maximus walked slowly towards the exit gate he was beginning to feel nervous about going on the plane. Would the plane take off with his weight on it? What about parachutes? Did they tell you how to use

them? What happened if the pilot didn't know the way?
You could get lost up in all those clouds without any
signposts.

'Excuse me, sir, but are you all right?' asked a pretty young air mousetress. 'You don't look very well.'

'I don't think I want to fly,' said Maximus. 'Mice weren't made to fly. The birds are best at it, we should leave it to them. I think I want to go home.'

'Is this your first flight ?' asked the air mousetress.
'Yes,' said Maximus.

Maximus felt a very small mouse after all his boasting about flying and going to America. He was very frightened and just wished he was at home in the vestry.

The air mousetress talked to Maximus about flying,

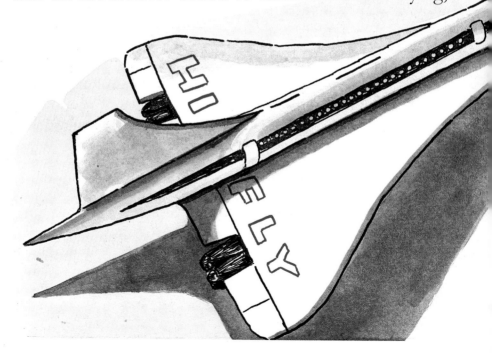

how safe it is to fly, how good the pilot was at finding his way, how everyone had a life jacket under his seat. She walked with him to the aeroplane and, at the top of the steps, introduced him to the friendly air mousetress who was on the flight.

Maximus was shown to his seat and had a wonderful view out of the window.

Maximus had a very exciting holiday in America. He visited all his cousins and in Disney World he saw the real Mickey Mouse. He went to Hollywood, met the

famous Jerry at the film studios and got his paw mark.
He even enjoyed the flight back home but when

Patrick, Paula and all the children met him at the
airport he thought carefully about boasting of it.

Heavenly Father,
Teach us that, whilst it is right to have pride in what we do,
it is not right to boast about it.
All our gifts come from you.
Help us to use them wisely in helping others for your sake.
Amen.